Icy Magic

Olivia the Octopus Fairy

BY
AANYA GARG

Pharos Books

Next book
in Icy Magic series
Catlyn the Clownfish Fairy

Paperback ISBN
9789355464163

©Publisher

Publisher: Pharos Books (P) Ltd.
Plot No.-55, Main Mother Dairy Road
Pandav Nagar, East Delhi-110092
Phone: 011-40395855, +14049995474
WhatsApp: +91 8368220032
E-mail: sales@pharosbooks.in
Website: www.pharosbooks.in
First Edition: 2022

Printed By: Sushma Book Binding House, Okhla
Industrial Area, Phase II, New Delhi-110020

Icy Magic: Oliva the Octopus Fairy
Aanya Garg

Books in Icy Magic Series

Ocean Fairies

Oceana the Ocean fairy

Anna the Anglerfish fairy

Sophia the Stonefish fairy

Olivia the Octopus fairy

Catlyn the Clownfish fairy

Rosella the Rockfish fairy

Molly the Manatee fairy

Dedicated to

My teachers

I appreciate your kindness, patience and all the hard work you put to make learning fun and exciting for me. You helped me become the person I am today. I owe you my lifelong respect.

CONTENTS

Each of the seven ocean fairies has a magical shell to keep the oceans in order. But Fireblast, a squawker, had stolen all the shells to create chaos in the oceans. The ocean fairies' powers are limited in the human world, that is why they took the help of two girls, Alice and Christy, to help them recover the shells. By placing their hands on a fairy when needed, the fairy's power increases. Thus far, only three shells have been found out of seven.

CHAPTER 1

Alice and Christy had joined a two-week summer camp at Coral Beach. It was the last day of their first week with Coral Adventures. The company had organized a surprise trip to The Underwater Sea Circus. From speed swimming

to jumps, turns and flips, kids would get to learn about amazingly athletic ocean animals in this thirty-minute show.

"Come on!" said Alice, "I don't want to miss a single bit of this Sea Circus show."

"Coming!" shouted back Christy. The show began with the dolphins performing aerial stunts followed by cute fluffy seals balancing balls on their noses. Then one of the octopuses did a spin in the air through a hoop. The crowd clapped and cheered. The top of the hoop was sparkling.

Alice and Christy took front seats for a closer look. They saw Olivia the Octopus Fairy sitting on top of the hoop. Their eyes lit up on seeing her, but they did not call out to her because that would draw unwanted attention to the fairy.

CHAPTER 2

Then another octopus with a purple hat came on stage and did a stunt, but it all went wrong. Alice and Christy noticed something weird about this octopus. They saw that it was holding a wand in one hand and a shell in another.

They knew it had to be Fireblast, who used the magic of the shell to disguise himself as an octopus. He was holding the opal shell.

The opal shell controls the ocean weather and helps keep the oceans calm. When nobody was looking, Olivia the Octopus Fairy fluttered from the

hoop and approached the girls. Olivia explained to them what could happen if the opal shell were misused.

She explained that the ocean water would become very turbulent. Ships would crash, sink and spill oil. Oil cannot dissolve in water. It forms a thin layer called oil slick floating on the water. Oil slicks can be very dangerous to sea animals, who will get poisoned if they swallow the oil.

CHAPTER
3

"We need to find the shell quickly," said Christy.

"Yes!" Alice and Olivia agreed. "But we have to think of a plan first."

"Look!" Olivia pointed. "That looks like the deadliest blue-ringed octopus there in the circus show.

This time we will get the blue-ringed octopus to chase Fireblast. Blue-ringed octopuses are the world's most venomous marine animals. They carry enough venom to kill 26 adult humans within minutes. It was pretty frightening for Fireblast to be chased by an anglerfish a few days ago.

It would be even more frightening to be chased by the blue-ringed octopus. Besides, octopuses are masters of camouflage. Their ability to match the colour of their surroundings allows them to hide in plain sight. Fireblast will not be able to see this threat coming to him."

CHAPTER 4

"But how do we call the blue-ringed octopus for help?" asked Alice and Christy in perplexed voices.

"Oh! I am Olivia the Octopus Fairy. The blue-

ringed octopus is my friend. When I blow my magical whistle, the octopus will hear its sound and come to me at once."

"Great!" said Alice. "Olivia, can you blow your whistle to call the octopus?"

"Yes, if you put your hands on me," Olivia nodded.

"Great! Then we will ask it to chase and sting Fireblast. When he gets stung, he will freeze and drop the shell. When the shell falls, your friend, the octopus, can dive down and get it back for us," suggested Alice excitedly.

"Perfect!" exclaimed Olivia. Then the girls placed their hands on Olivia's shoulders. Drawing energy from human contact, Olivia blew the

magical whistle. Nobody noticed the blue-ringed

octopus coming to Alice and Christy as people in

the show were too busy cheering and enjoying the

spins of the sea animals. Olivia whispered the plan

to the octopus.

CHAPTER
5

The blue-ringed octopus ran straight back to the pool and chased the octopus with the purple hat carrying the wand and the shell. The blue-ringed octopus tried to catch him but other sea creatures and octopuses were getting in its way.

Finally, it touched the octopus with the purple hat with its pointy tip. Fireblast shook, froze and revealed his true self. The blue-ringed octopus managed to grab Fireblast with its two hands and snatched the shell from him.

It swam back up to the surface of the water and threw the shell to Christy and Alice.

Before Alice and Christy could catch the shell, Fireblast leapt high in the air and grabbed it in his hand. He then blew hot winds at them.

Olivia responded by throwing a frost ball which hit Fireblast right on his head, freezing him into a statue.

The octopus hurriedly swooped down and snatched the shell from his hand and passed it to Alice. Alice further passed the shell to Olivia who then quickly touched the shell with the tip of her wand, taking the three of them to the Icy Palace.

"Hello!" said the king and the queen in lovely voices.

"We've got the opal shell back," said Olivia.

`"Great!" said the queen, keeping the shell back in the chest. "Once again, you have saved the lives of ocean animals."

Fireblast had stolen the magical shells that belonged to the ocean fairies. Alice and Christy managed to find four of them. Four are still missing. Do you think they will be able to get them as well? Read on in Catlyn the Catfish Fairy.

FUN FACTS ABOUT OCTOPUS

DO YOU KNOW!

Octopuses are ocean creatures that are striking for having eight arms and bulb-like heads.

Three hearts

An octopus has three hearts.

Size

They come in different sizes. The common octopus is 12 to 36 inches long and weighs 3 to 10 kg. The giant Pacific octopus is the largest octopus species. It generally grows to 16 feet long and weighs around 50 kg. The largest one was recorded to weigh more than 272 kg and to reach 30 feet in length. The smallest octopus is the Octopus wolfi. It is less than an inch (2.5 cm) and weighs less than a gram.

Life Span

Octopuses have short life spans. Some species only live for around six months. Other species, like the North Pacific giant octopus can live as long as five years. Typically, the larger the octopus, the longer it lives.

Blue Blood

Octopus blood is blue. This because the blood contains a copper-based protein called hemocyanin.

They are boneless

Being boneless, they can squeeze into and out of tight spaces.

Habitat

Octopuses live in oceans all over the world. Generally, they live near the water's surface in shells, reefs and crevices. Some species live on the floor of the ocean, making their homes out of caves.

Diet

Octopuses are carnivores. They eat clams, shrimp, lobsters, fish, sharks and even birds.

How they catch their prey

When threatened, octopuses will shoot a dark liquid, sometimes called ink, at their predator. This will temporarily blind and confuse a potential attacker, giving the octopus time to swim away. The ink can also dull the attacker's smelling and tasting abilities.

FUN FACTS ABOUT BLUE-RINGED OCTOPUS

About blue-ringed octopus

It is one of the deadliest underwater creatures and is only 2-4 inches (5-10 cm) in length and weighs 0.2 lb (80 g).

What do blue-ringed octopuses look like?

They have bright blue rings that cover their body and the colour of the skin may range from yellow ochre and light brown.

What do they eat?

The greater blue-ringed octopus is a carnivore and it preys on crabs, molluscs, and fishes.

How long does a greater blue-ringed octopus live?

The lifespan of a greater blue-ringed octopus is approximately two to three years.

Are they dangerous?

They are extremely dangerous. However, a blue-ringed octopus does not attack immediately. Once it senses a threat, it flashes its shimmery blue ring as an alarm as a warning. However, if the threat persists, it will release its venom, tetrodotoxin, which can kill humans. It carries enough poison to 26 adults, all within a few minutes.

Where does a greater blue-ringed octopus live?

It lives in the shallow waters of the Indian and Pacific Ocean, amongst the coral reefs and tidal pools, in areas ranging from the Philippines to Sri Lanka and Papua New Guinea to the coasts of Australia.

HELP OLIVIA FIND HER SHELL

TRUE/FALSE

1. Alice and Christy met Olivia at snow city.

2. The Opal shell controls the ocean weather and helps keep oceans calm.

3. Fireblast disguised himself as a fairy.

4. Olivia touched the shell with the tip of her wand.

5. Blue-ringed octopuses are the world's most venomous marine animals.

Answers- 1) False, 2) True, 3) False, 4) True, 5) True

My special thanks to:

My editor, Li Ping, who edited my books with her usual fine eye to details. Her expertise and advice have been invaluable.

My illustrator, Aru Sharma, who designed my book with patience and panache and rendered beautiful book cover and illustrations.

Released Already!

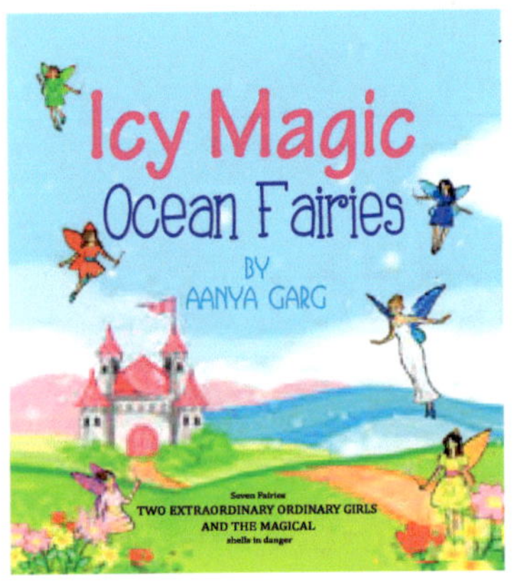

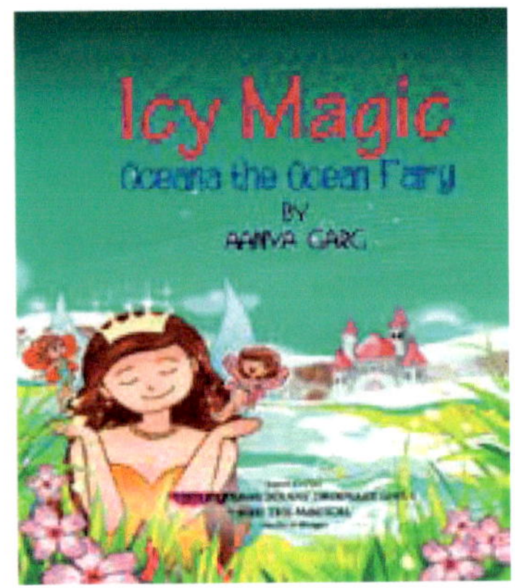

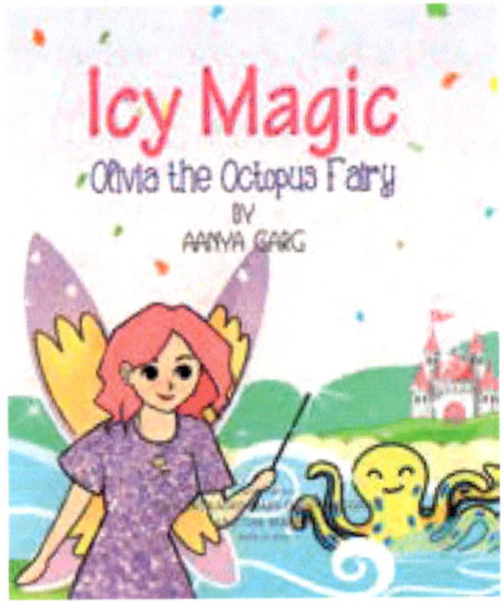

Next book in Icy Magic series
Catlyn the Clownfish fairy